Printed in the United States of America

ISBN: 978-0578590141

Pedee Creek Press
www.brohagan.com

PRESENTING

JONATHAN MARVEL'S

CHRISTMAS
POCKETS

B. R. O'HAGAN

This is the message of Christmas:
We are never alone.

onathan Marvel's mother and father raced through the double doors beneath the red EMERGENCY sign. In the waiting room a table with a small Christmas tree and a ceramic Nativity scene separated three rows of unoccupied plastic chairs from the admitting desk and the wide tile corridors that lead into the hospital.

Mrs. Marvel clutched her husband's arm as they walked to the desk. At that moment, a double-wide door marked 'No Admittance' swung open, and a police officer hurried in their direction.

"I'm Officer Murdock," she said. "Are you the Marvels?"

Mr. Marvel nodded. His wife looked anxiously at the officer.

"Jonathan—my son—where is he? Is he alright? Can we see him?"

Officer Murdock motioned to two chairs. "Sit down, please," she said. "I'll let them know that you're here." She went to the desk and spoke with the nurse. She pointed over to the Marvels and then came over to where they sat.

"Jonathan is in surgery," said the officer. "The paramedics brought him in about 45 minutes ago. We found this in his jeans pocket."

She handed Mrs. Marvel the laminated card with their home contact information that Jonathan carried when he was out and about.

"I don't understand," said Mr. Marvel. "He's in surgery? What happened? Why is he here? How is he? When can we see him?"

Officer Murdock slid a plastic chair across the carpet and sat down in front of the Marvels. "Jonathan was in an accident," she said. "He stepped off the curb into traffic in front of Yee's grocery. He was hit by a delivery truck."

Jonathan's mother clapped her hand across her mouth. His father clenched the arms of his plastic chair.

"Hit by a truck," he said slowly, shaking his head from side to side. "I don't understand. A truck hit him? Were they running a red light? Were they drunk? Is the driver in jail?"

He turned to his wife and repeated, "Hit by a truck. Jonathan."

She blinked back tears.

The Officer shook her head. "I was only a few yards away when it happened. I saw it all. Your son stepped into the street without looking at the lights. He was distracted…patting all of those"–she looked for the right word–"those odd-looking pockets on the front of that big overcoat of his."

"The crosswalk light was still red but he stepped right off the curb and into oncoming traffic. The driver of the truck was too close. He couldn't stop. He tried to pull to the left but the right front corner of his bumper clipped Jonathan and threw him hard against the curb."

She leaned forward towards the Marvels and in a quiet voice added, "Jonathan's head hit the curb. I got to him in seconds. He was bleeding and unconscious. We had him here in less than five minutes. They're doing all they–they're taking good care of him."

Jonathan's father swallowed hard. Mrs. Marvel wrapped her arms tightly against her chest.

"What was he doing there," she said in a whisper. "None of his friends live by the Yee's. It's three blocks from our home. He's only eight, for heaven's sake. He's not allowed to just wander." Her voiced trailed off.

"You said he was wearing a big overcoat with 'odd' pockets," said Mr. Marvel. "What do you mean?"

"You know," replied the officer. "All those different colored patch pockets on that big coat. I don't think I've ever seen anything like it."

Just then Jonathan's grandmother bustled into the waiting room. Mrs. Marvel held her in a long hug. When a nurse in green hospital scrubs appeared from a side door and looked around the room Officer Murdock motioned her over. Mr. Marvel stood up, and the little group formed a semi-circle in front of the nurse.

"Jonathan will be in surgery for a while," said the nurse. "We were fortunate that Dr. Wise, who is a pediatric neurosurgeon from the capitol, was here this afternoon to do a seminar for our surgical staff. When Jonathan was brought in to Emergency, Dr. Wise was actually in the next room. He was told about your son and he scrubbed right in alongside our team."

The nurse looked at Jonathan's parents. "Your son is in excellent hands."

Mr. and Mrs. Marvel both started to speak at the same time.

"How is he? What kind of surgery? How soon will it be over? What's usual in cases like this?

"The doctor will come and speak with you when surgery is complete," said the nurse. "He'll answer all of your questions and if there are any updates along the way I will come out and tell you." She placed one hand on Mrs. Marvel's forearm, and said, "A lot of very skilled and caring people are with your son right now. I'll see you soon."

The nurse turned and pushed through the doors that led into the surgical area.

Grandmother Marvel pointed to the small cross on the wall above the door.

"Caring people," she said to no one in particular. "I'm so very glad."

With that she sank into a chair and pulled a tissue from her purse.

An hour passed. Mr. Marvel met with the admitting staff and filled out what felt like an endless stack of forms. Their Pastor arrived, followed moments later by Mr. and Mrs. Yee, who owned the little grocery store at the site of Jonathan's accident.

Mr. Yee had a sack of cookies and donuts, Mrs. Yee carried jugs of coffee and hot chocolate. As the late afternoon sun flooded the waiting room the Pastor rounded up cups and helped to serve.

Mr. Marvel returned from the admitting desk. He shook Pastor's hand and gratefully accepted a donut and coffee from Mrs. Yee.

"It's very kind of you to come," he said to the Yees.

"We are so sorry about Jonathan," said Mrs. Yee.

"And we always close on Christmas Eve afternoon," added her husband. "So, no problem for our business."

Mrs. Marvel shot a glance at her husband. He understood. They knew the Yees did not close their store on Christmas Eve, or any other day of the year.

The Pastor went over to the Nativity scene and adjusted a few of the ceramic figures. "I'd almost forgotten what day it was," he said. "Imagine that." He looked around the waiting area, which was empty except for Jonathan's family and friends. "Not the busiest day of the year for hospitals, it seems."

The little group spoke in hushed whispers. Grandmother Marvel had a bag of crochet supplies and Mrs. Yee sat down beside her to watch as she brought a small decorative doily to life stitch-by-stitch.

As Mr. Marvel was pulling a sweater around his wife's shoulders a few minutes after 6:00 PM the 'No Admittance' door opened. The nurse who had spoken with them earlier came out followed by a tall man dressed in surgical green from the coverings on his shoes to the cap on his head.

Mr. Marvel grabbed his wife's hand and leapt to his feet. Grandmother and the rest of the group formed a line behind them. The doctor shook the Marvels' hands and introduced himself. His eyes were steady and his voice was calm and assuring but his news was very frightening.

"Jonathan is a strong boy," he began. "And that's the best thing going for him. He took quite a blow on the head. He suffered a subdural hematoma, which is what happens when blood collects between the layers of tissue that surround the brain. The bleeding is under the skull and outside the brain, not in the brain itself."

The doctor paused, waiting to make sure that the Marvels were following his explanation. "As blood accumulates," he continued, "pressure on the brain increases. The pressure on the brain is our concern in these cases. If pressure inside the skull rises to very high level and we are not able to reduce it a subdural hematoma can be fatal."

Mrs. Marvel's face went blank. Her husband held her arm and the Pastor stood behind them and placed a hand on each of their shoulders.

Grandmother dropped her crochet needle on the floor and the Yees took a few steps back to give the family privacy.

"The procedure we just completed has reduced the swelling and pressure—for now," said the surgeon. "We're going to be monitoring him very closely. A nurse will be sitting beside his bed for the next several hours. "

Mr. Marvel took a deep breath. He had to ask the question. But before he could form the words the doctor anticipated what was coming and answered without hesitation.

"Jonathan is a very sick little boy. He has suffered a terrible injury. But the brain is a remarkable organ; it's resilient and tough and so is he."

The doctor stepped closer to the Marvels and took their hands in his. He nodded in the direction of the cross above the surgical department entry. "This is a very special place," he said. "And today is a special day. I will see you both a little later."

He turned to go, then turned back. "I have to ask you about that coat he was wearing," said the doctor. "All those funny pockets stuffed with something—the paramedics said it was so well padded that it actually helped to cushion his fall—probably saved him from some broken ribs. I saw it at the nurse's station; I have to tell you I've never seen anything like it."

Mr. Marvel shook his head. "That's the second time today someone has mentioned Jonathan's coat. We have no idea where it came from or what's in it. Seems to be the mystery of the day."

The doctor smiled. "Whatever the story behind that coat may be,- today was the right day for Jonathan to be wearing it."

The Marvels returned to their chairs and to the waiting that stretched into forever. Pastor sat beside them scribbling notes for the Christmas sermon he would be giving the next morning. Mr. Yee announced that he was going to go and get some snacks, but at just that moment the entry door slid open and a women stepped in carrying three large, white sacks.

"I didn't know how many people might be here so I pretty much cleaned them out," said Officer Murdock, who had changed into civilian clothes.

Mr. Yee pulled a table in front of the Marvels, and Officer Murdock pulled hamburgers, fries, and sodas from the bags. Mrs. Marvel shook her head.

"Afraid I have to insist on this one, honey," said her husband, placing some food in front of his wife. "You have to stay strong. It could be a long night."

Jonathan's family and friends visited as they ate. Officer Murdock, who was off duty, asked about Jonathan, and Mrs. Marvel found it made her feel a bit better to tell stories about her energetic, imaginative eight year-old son and all of his adventures.

"Do you think that coat everyone is talking about had anything to do with one of those adventures?" asked Officer Murdock.

Mrs. Marvel smiled for the first time that day. "Oh, I have a feeling he was up to something," she said. "And when he gets better we're going to have a chat about finding adventures that don't include him running all over town."

As they talked a hospital cleaning woman maneuvered her cart around the waiting room, wiping down plastic chairs, dusting surfaces, cleaning glass. When she was done she parked the cart near the reception desk and came over to the Marvels.

"Excuse me," she said in broken English. "I know you. My son Felipe is in Jonathan's class at school."

"Sure, I recognize you from parent's meetings," said Mrs. Marvel.

The cleaning woman smiled. "I don't go to as many as I would like. I work nights. It's just Felipe and me at my home."

Mrs. Marvel nodded.

"When I heard about your son I called Felipe and asked him to go across the street from our apartment to St. Thomas church and light a candle."

She waited a moment, but Mrs. Marvel did not respond. "I just wanted you to know," she said. She put her hands in her pockets and walked away.

Grandmother Marvel touched her daughter-in-laws' arm and nodded in the cleaning woman's direction. Mrs. Marvel put a hamburger and fries on a paper plate, picked up a soda and went across the room. She gave the food to Felipe's mother and then leaned against the wall while the cleaning woman ate her meal. The two mothers talked about their boys for several minutes.

Mrs. Yee was cleaning up the paper plates a little after 9:00 when the ER nurse came out to get the Marvels. "You can see Jonathan for just a minute," she said.

Mrs. Marvel held her husband's hand tightly as they followed the nurse towards the surgical recovery area. When they passed through the door Mr. Marvel paused for a moment and looked up towards the cross. He bowed his head, put his arm around his wife's shoulder, and walked her back to see their son.

When they returned a few minutes later the Marvels sat back down on their hard plastic chairs without saying a word.

"Honey," Grandmother Marvel finally said.

Mrs. Marvel raised her head. She realized that while they were inside the recovery room two more people had come to the hospital. Jonathan's teacher was sitting on a chair a few rows away talking with the cleaning woman. Sitting in a corner by herself was Jonathan's teenage babysitter.

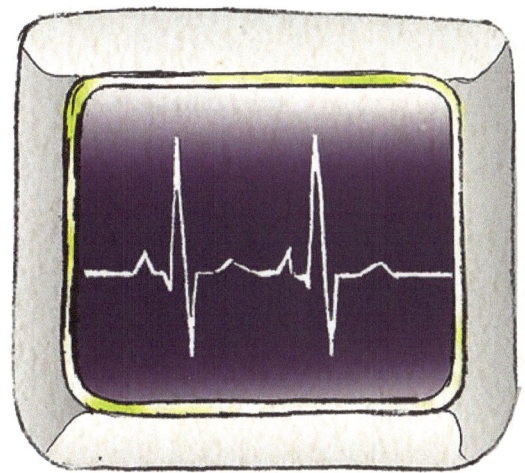

Mrs. Marvel asked the Pastor to bring everyone over. When they were all gathered around, she looked at her husband to see if he wanted to tell them about Jonathan. But he remained silent, his hands clasped in his lap, staring at the floor.

Mrs. Marvel said, "Jonathan is sleeping. There are so many machines and wires and tubes and bandages. We could barely make him out in the middle of all of it. A nurse is sitting beside him. His face, it's…his face is.."

Her voice quieted to a whisper.

Mr. Marvel looked up. His voice sounded faraway. "It's terribly swollen. He needs a respirator to breathe." What more was there to say?

Jonathan's babysitter and teacher moved their chairs closer to the rest of the group. Conversations would begin, and then stop quickly any time a door opened. Officer Murdock went outside to talk with two paramedics who had come to the ER for supplies. While she was outside, a rumpled old man came through the door and looked around the room.

"Oh, my gosh," said Mrs. Marvel. "Honey look, it's Mr. Cowl, from down the street."

The old man caught sight of them, and came across the room. A moment later the surliest curmudgeon in the neighborhood—the one that parents avoided and children feared—was standing right in front of the Marvels.

"Is it true your boy was hurt?" asked the old man.

"I'm afraid so, Mr. Cowl," Jonathan's father replied. "He's in a recovery room now. We're waiting. We're hopeful."

"That's an awful thing," said Mr. Cowl. "Just awful."

The old man could not find any other words to say. He shifted from one foot to the other until Pastor ended the awkward moment by suggesting they get some coffee. He had always wanted a chance to talk with the famous old gentleman.

"I didn't know Mr. Cowl knew Jonathan," said Mrs. Marvel.

"I'm beginning to think there's a lot we don't know about our little boy," her husband replied. "Look around the room. His teacher is here and so is his babysitter. His grandmother is with us of course, and our Pastor. A police officer is here even though she doesn't know us, and on her time off, too. Even the neighborhood grocers are here. The hospital cleaning woman turns out to be the mother of one of Jonathan's pals, and, who is that with her?"

They hadn't noticed a young boy about Jonathan's age coming into the waiting area. He was talking to the cleaning woman across the room.

"I'm sure that must be her son," said Mrs. Marvel.

"We make for quite a group don't we," said Mr. Marvel. "And each one of us praying for our boy."

Mrs. Marvel managed a tired smile. She squeezed her husband's arm, and said, "Even Mr. Cowl?"

He looked across the room where his grumpy neighbor was engaged in what appeared to be a rather spirited conversation with the Pastor.

"You know," said Mr. Marvel, "I think so. Even Mr. Cowl."

Mr. Marvel accepted a cup of water from Mrs. Yee, and then told his wife he was going to join the Pastor and Mr. Cowl. As he stood up the ER nurse returned to the waiting room. She motioned for the Marvels to come over by themselves. The room fell silent. All eyes were on the nurse as she huddled with the Marvels. The nurse gave them each a hug and then disappeared behind the door beneath the 'No Admittance' sign.

When the Marvels walked back to their chairs the weight of the world was piled on their shoulders. Mrs. Marvel collapsed in her chair, sobbing. Grandmother sat quietly beside her and held her hand.

Mr. Marvel motioned for everyone to come close. In a few seconds he was surrounded by family, friends, and even a few people who until a few short hours ago had been complete strangers. He felt closer to this small group than any people he had ever known.

"Jonathan is back in surgery," he said at last. "The first procedure did not stop the swelling of his brain. They're very concerned now that they may not be able to control it, or, even if they can, they don't know if they can prevent permanent damage being done to his brain function."

He looked at the large clock on the wall above the Nativity scene. It was 10:10 PM. A door on the other side of the surgical area entryway opened, and the faint sounds of a Christmas carol drifted their way. Then the door closed.

The people waiting on Christmas Eve to hear the news about Jonathan Marvel broke up into small clusters around the room. A nurse brought out a fresh pot of coffee, and Mrs. Yee made her rounds once again. Grandmother Marvel sat with Jonathan's babysitter and showed her how to crochet, while Jonathan's teacher talked with Felipe and his mother, who was now off work.

Mr. Yee joined Mr. Cowl and the Pastor as they returned to their lively conversation and Officer Murdock stepped out of the waiting room.

The surgery door opened, and an unfamiliar nurse came into the waiting room. She was carrying a thick, multi-colored bundle. The receptionist pointed to the Marvels and the nurse brought the bundle to them. Mrs. Marvel spread it out on her lap.

"So this is the coat everyone has been talking about all day," she said to her husband. "It's that horrible old overcoat of yours that I tossed into the trash weeks ago. And the pockets, honey, look at the pockets."

Mr. Marvel did not have to be told to look. You couldn't miss them. They covered the front of the coat from just below the shoulders to an inch or so above the hem on both sides of the zipper.

"Oh, my goodness, look at those," said Grandmother. "And that boy made them."

"Well that explains what happened to my tape," said Mr. Marvel. "I've been looking for it for days."

"That blue pocket?" said Mrs. Mrs. Marvel. "That was my best new dishcloth! Jonathan you rascal, what have you been up to?"

As they unfolded the coat and examined its crazy quilt of mismatched pockets everyone in the room gathered around. The bulging multi-colored pockets made for quite an unusual sight.

Jonathan's teacher was the first to notice the labels. "Those small strips of masking tape on the pockets," she said. "Is that writing on them?"

Mr. Marvel looked closely. "Yes, it is. It's in pencil, and pretty faint, but it sure is Jonathan's printing."

"What do they say?" asked the babysitter.

Mrs. Marvel lifted one corner of the coat for a closer look. "This one says, 'For Grandmother Marvel.'"

"Oh, my," said Grandmother. "For me?"

"And this one says 'For Mr. and Mrs. Yee,'" continued Jonathan's mother.

The Yees shared a quizzical glance. A pocket for them?

"This pocket label says it's for you," said Mr. Marvel to his wife.

She pointed to her former dishrag. "And this one is for you. At least it died for a good cause. "

"What on earth," said the Pastor.

"That's a good question, since this red pocket has your name on it," said Mr. Marvel.

"And there is a pocket here for Jonathan's babysitter, and one for his teacher, too," continued Mrs. Marvel.

Jonathan's teacher took the babysitter's hand. What on earth, indeed? "There is a pocket here for Felipe, and one for his mother," said Mr. Marvel. "And this one, the biggest one, says it's for the baby Jesus."

The Pastor seemed pleased with the announcement of that label, while Felipe just looked astonished to hear his name mentioned. His mother stood behind him, her hands resting on his shoulders.

"Are there more?" asked Grandmother.

"Yes, two more," said Mrs. Marvel. "This one says, oh my gosh: it says 'Give this one to Mr. Cowl, even if he doesn't want it.'"

Old Mr. Cowl had been standing at the edge of the group as each name was read aloud. He snapped around when he heard his name and every eye in the room was on him—something he was really not used to.

He gave his best 'get-off-my-lawn' scowl, and said, "What? I don't know what this is all about."

Mrs. Marvel turned to her husband. "Should we open the pockets and hand out whatever is inside?"

"I think we better," he said. "It's pretty clear that Jonathan was getting ready to deliver these to everybody himself. I guess that all these pockets just made more sense to him than carrying everything around in a couple grocery bags."

Mr. Marvel raised his voice. "Please, everybody," he said. "Pull your chairs around in a circle."

It took a minute to get everyone arranged and a special plea from Grandmother Marvel to get Mr. Cowl to join the group. Felipe held back, choosing to stand behind his mother's chair.

"Jonathan's accident happened in front of Yee's grocery," said Mr. Marvel. "I think we can assume he was headed there first." With that, he dipped into the pocket marked 'Mr. & Mrs. Yee,' and pulled out a folded, 9"x12" brown craft paper envelope. He handed it to his wife, who carried it over to the Yee's.

Mr. Yee accepted the envelope gingerly, as though he was receiving a sacred relic. His wife nodded and he unfolded the envelope and tore it open. Ten sets of eyes were glued on him as he pulled out the items one by one.

First out was a small plastic sandwich bag. Mr. Yee held it up for everyone to see.

"Looks like macadamia nuts," he said. He reached in again- and pulled out a shiny blue tri-fold brochure. He handed it to his wife who read the headline: "Relax in Tropical Tahiti."

She looked mystified. Tahiti? What did a tropical island have to do with her and her husband?

"Is that everything in the envelope?" asked the Pastor.

Mr. Yee reached inside. "No," he said, "one more thing here. A piece of paper."

He unfolded the sheet of paper, which everyone could see was heavily decorated with orange and green palm trees. Mrs. Marvel recognized Jonathan's printing.

"Mr. Yee, would you mind reading what it says?" she asked.

"Of course, of course." Mr. Yee pulled a pair of reading glasses out of his jacket pocket and began to read:

Dear Mr. & Mrs. Yee

First of all, Merry Christmas. I don't know if you have Christmas where you are from but it is my favorite time of the year. I like coming to your store and nobody has better comics than you and you let me read them sometimes without telling me I have to buy them, so I hope lots of people buy them at your store.

Mrs. Yee beamed and nodded her head at the compliment. Her husband continued:

My dad told me that nobody in the world works harder than you do, and he said you don't ever take vacations, you work all the time. So I heard in school about this place called Tahiti and it looks like someplace you could get some rest. I wish I could get you tickets there, but all I could get you were some nuts that come from somewhere around there. I hope you like them and can have a vacation sometime.

Your friend,

Jonathan Marvel

Mr. Yee folded the paper to put it away and then thought better of it and handed it across to Mrs. Marvel. She held it to her chest and shook her head with a smile.

"Honey," she said to her husband, "you'd better get all of those passed out pretty fast. I don't think I can take this."

Soft laughter rippled through the group.

"Ok, then," said Mr. Marvel. He opened another pocket and pulled out a folded envelope. "This one is for you, Pastor."

The Pastor took the envelope, and following the Yee's example, opened it and examined the contents. "No snacks for me," he said, "I was kind of hoping for that." He held up a sheet of paper filled with Jonathan's clean block printing. He cleared his throat and read:

Hello Pastor. Merry Christmas, too. It was hard to think of something to give you because my mom says you are a special friend of God's and that kind of sounds like about the coolest thing of all. So, I was thinking and I asked my dad what you maybe needed and my dad said that "what Pastor needs are some new ideas for his sermons; his old stories are getting a little stale."

The Pastor gave Mr. Marvel a funny 'why-I-oughta' stare. Mr. Marvel flushed but everyone else laughed, even old Mr. Cowl.

"If I may continue?" said Pastor. "What Jonathan has done here is to list his three top ideas for new sermons. Here they are."

Number 1: Please tell more stories about David & Goliath and guys like them. Nobody could fall asleep listening about all those battles, and besides, we wouldn't mind if you told them over and over again.

Number 2: Could you maybe give some of those Bible people different names? When I hear names like Aberniddydilledop it's confusing. If you want some help I could think up some better names that people can remember.

Number 3: Sometimes when we leave church, the things you talked about make me feel like I want to go and do some stuff to help other people. But I'm only 8, so I don't know what kind of things to do. You are really good at helping people, so maybe sometime you could talk about stuff that kids can do to help people, too. OK, those are my ideas. Merry Christmas, Jonathan.

P.S.: I know if you talk about more cool battles they had in olden times that my dad won't plug in his little radio to listen to the game during church.

The Pastor removed his glasses and wiped his eyes with his sleeve. "30 years in the pulpit," he said as he handed the letter to Mrs. Marvel, "and those are some of the best sermon ideas I have ever heard."

Mrs. Marvel smiled as she took the letter, folded it over and rapped her husband on the head with it. She got the smile she wanted from him—and another laugh from the group.

Mr. Marvel reached into the third pocket. Inside was an object about the size of a stick of butter, wrapped in newspaper.

He stood up and carried it over to Jonathan's teacher.

Her eyes began to tear up, which earned her a, "Oh, no you don't, or we'll never get through this," from Mrs. Marvel.

The teacher chuckled and unwrapped the package. Inside was a huge pencil eraser and a note. She read:

You always say that by the time we get through life we will make about a million mistakes. Since you are still pretty young you have lots of mistakes to go. I hope this helps. Your student in the second row, Jonathan Marvel.

Erase Away

As the teacher finished sharing the gift from her pocket, Officer Murdock and the babysitter circulated through the group with a tray of cookies.

"Who's next?" asked Grandmother.

Mr. Marvel glanced at the clock. It was 11:30. He opened another pocket.

"Felipe, this is for you," he said

Jonathan's classmate didn't budge. Instead, he balled up his fists at his side and stared defiantly at the ground. His mother left her chair and took the small padded envelope from Mr. Marvel. She returned to her seat and opened the package. Inside was a tiny soft cover book, about 4 inches by 4 inches. Felipe's mom held it up for everyone to see. Even Felipe shot a quick glance at the cover.

Felipe's mom read the title: *"100 Really Cool Things For Boys To Do."* She opened the cover and slowly read what Jonathan had written on the title page:

Dear Felipe,
I wish you were my friend because you are the best soccer player in our class. But it seems like you are mad all the time and maybe you don't want any friends at this school.
Did you have friends at your old school? Maybe we could do some of the stuff in this book, like on the page where they tell you how to build an old-time tree-house fort. There is a big tree in my yard if you want to build one with me.
I sit right behind you in class, if you don't remember me. So come to my house anytime, except when we have to go to church.
My name is Jonathan Marvel.

Felipe's mom finished reading and handed the book to her son. He took it grudgingly, but after a moment he was flipping though the pages.

"There he goes with the church stuff again," laughed the Pastor. "I'd better get that new David & Goliath sermon done in a hurry."

As Mr. Marvel reached into another pocket on the old overcoat, the door to the waiting room slid open. Officer Murdock was back, accompanied by a very tired looking middle-aged man in workman's clothing. They went up to the reception desk before settling on two chairs on the other side of the large room.

"The next package is for Felipe's mother," said Mr. Marvel. His wife unrolled the long, thin, tissue-wrapped gift and took it to Felipe's mother. She hesitated. A few hours ago she was cleaning this very room and these people were strangers to her and her son. Now, even in the midst of the pain and uncertainty about Jonathan Marvels' condition as he underwent his second surgery, she felt warmer and more welcome than she had since she and her son moved here a year ago.

She opened Jonathan's note and read:

Hi Felipe's mom,

I heard Felipe tell our teacher that you couldn't come to Open House night because you had to clean a lot of stuff everyday at a hospital. He said you did manual labor, and I didn't know what that was so I asked my dad and he said that is work you do with your hands.

So, this is for your hands and I hope it helps.

Merry Christmas from Jonathan Marvel.

And P.S., I am in Felipe's class. He is a cool guy.

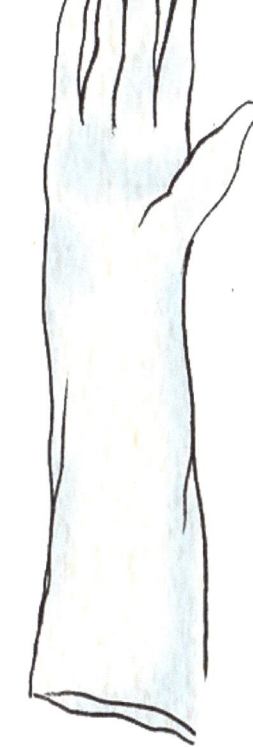

Felipe's mother dug through the layers of tissue paper. Inside was a pair of white evening gloves, the kind that go up almost to the elbow. Grandmother Marvel looked over at her daughter-in-law with an expression that said "weren't those mine years and years ago?"

Felipe's mother couldn't help but laugh. She quickly caught herself but it was too late: a moment later everyone in the little circle of chairs surrounding Mr. and Mrs. Marvel and their son's ridiculous-looking coat began to laugh. Mrs. Marvel laughed so hard she began to cry. They made such a racket that the nurse at the reception desk slid her window closed.

"Oh, honey," Mrs. Marvel said to her husband, "I don't even know what to say. That little boy of ours." Then she got up and gave Felipe's mother a hug.

"Anytime you want to borrow these, let me know," said Felipe's mother, which set Mrs. Marvel laughing once again.

The doors to the surgery hadn't opened in over an hour.

"Next pocket?" asked Jonathan's teacher.

Mr. Marvel opened another pocket, and pulled out a battered green book. "This is for Mr. Cowl."

The old man shook his head from side to side. "I don't think so, no I don't believe I will," he said. "Just open another pocket. I'll pass."

"I can't do that Mr. Cowl," said Jonathan's father. "The label on the pocket says to give it to you even if you don't want it. I would really appreciate if you would take it. It's pretty clear you are important to him." Mr. Marvel didn't have to complete his thought. Everyone in the group was thinking the same thing at that moment: "You must be important to Jonathan, but we don't know why."

Mr. Cowl shifted in his seat. This was the most social interaction he had experienced in longer than he could remember. It was difficult for him. But it was for the boy, and the little fellow did sometimes pick the newspaper off the sidewalk and drop it on his stoop, and he always waved when he walked past the house.

Mr. Cowl was also fairly certain that it had been Jonathan who had left a bag of assorted candy on his porch the day after Halloween.

The note on the bag was not signed. It said, "My mom said I can't have this much candy, but I bet you can if you want to."

The man known throughout the neighborhood as Mr. B.A. Grump shrugged his shoulders in resignation. He took the beaten-up book from Mr. Marvel's hand, stuck it in his jacket pocket, and sat back down.

"No, Mr. Cowl, now that's not at all fair," said the Pastor. "Everyone has opened their gift from Jonathan and read his message. Please—share yours with us."

The old man knew when he was beat. He just wanted to get this over with. He pulled the book from his jacket. "The title," he began…

"Please, speak up," said Mr. Yee. "We can't hear you."

Mr. Cowl coughed, and started again. His voice was loud and clear this time.

"The title is, '*A Boy's Book of Jokes*.'"

"And the inscription?" asked Grandmother Marvel.

"Humph," mumbled the old man. He flipped to the opening page and read.

Dear Mr. Cowl,

How are you? Did you like that candy? Everybody says you are really, really old…

Another "humph" flew from Mr. Cowl's lips. But he went on:

…really old, so I thought you might like something as old as you are. Do you like jokes? I do. My mom told me that your wife died and that is why you don't like people anymore. Sometimes when I feel that way I read my joke book. OK, things don't always get better when I read, but it sure is fun to laugh sometimes.

So I hope you laugh at these jokes and if you want me to come over with my joke book sometime I can show you the really funny ones I like and you can read me the ones in your book that make you laugh.

Merry Christmas,

Jonathan Marvel, the joke-teller

Mr. Cowl turned the book over in his hands. "Joke-teller, huh? Well now, I believe I just might read a few of these."

He slipped the book back into his jacket, and nodded a thank-you to the Marvels.

Jonathan Marvel's Christmas pockets were emptying quickly. "You next," said Mrs. Marvel to Jonathan's babysitter. The babysitter stood while she opened her package. She was a quiet, shy girl who the Marvels knew had few friends. She was good with Jonathan and responsible with her babysitting duties.

Inside the pocket with her name was an electric blue wrap-around scarf. She looped it several times around her neck and then read Jonathan's message:

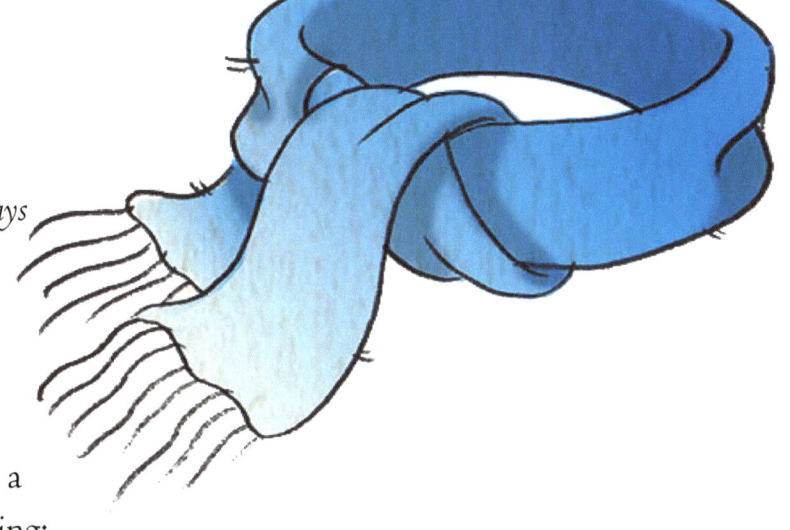

You are the best babysitter, and I don't even feel bad about needing a babysitter because you are so much fun. But the only thing I don't know is how come you always say you aren't pretty, because you are really pretty I think.

The babysitter's cheeks turned scarlet, but she managed a small laugh, and continued reading:

Mom says anytime she doesn't feel pretty she goes shopping for something new. So I saved my money from chores and got this scarf and it is completely new. Now put it on, and people will tell you that you're really pretty.

Merry Christmas from Jonathan.

Felipe's mom was the first to say, "You really are a lovely girl."

"That color is just right for you," said Jonathan's teacher.

"Be sure and wear it to school," added Mrs. Marvel. "Everyone will notice you."

The lights in the waiting room flickered. Mr. Marvel noted that it was ten minutes to midnight. To Christmas. He wrapped his arm around his wife's shoulder and pulled her close

"It's almost Christmas," he whispered.

"I know," she said. "I can't imagine Christmas morning without him running down the stairs. I just can't."

Mr. Marvel had never lied to his wife. He hoped he wasn't lying now when he said to her, "I promise you. Jonathan will run down our stairs next Christmas, and the Christmas after that and every Christmas as long as we are together. Do you hear me?"

The Marvels family and friends gave them their moment. Everyone was aware that only a few feet from where they sat Jonathan Marvel was fighting for his life. If only an answer to their prayer could be found in one of his Christmas pockets.

The Pastor brought them back to the task at hand. "Only a few pockets left to open," he said to the Marvels. "What would you like to do?"

"My wife and I have decided to wait until Jonathan comes home," said Mr. Marvel. "That's where he intended to give them to us. That's where we will open them."

"That goes for me as well," added Grandmother. "I want that boy to see the expression on my face when I open his gift."

"Then that leaves just two pockets," said the Pastor.

"One is for the baby Jesus," said Mrs. Marvel. She took a small box wrapped in aluminum foil from its pocket and handed it to the Pastor. "Would you please give it to Him?"

"It will be a privilege for me, and baby Jesus," said the Pastor.

Mr. Marvel asked for everyone's attention. "I can't begin to tell each of you what it means to my wife and me to have you here with us tonight," he said.

His wife nodded.

"It's almost Christmas," he continued. "Just five minutes away. But there is one pocket on Jonathan's coat that has my wife and I baffled. There's no name on it, so my guess is that Jonathan hadn't found that person yet today. The label says it is for the one person Jonathan would meet today who needed a gift the most. I'm not sure what that means."

He held up an envelope. "It looks like there is a letter of some kind inside. Maybe you all can help figure out who needs a gift the most today."

Mr. Marvel scooted his chair closer to the group and asked the Pastor to invite Officer Murdock to join them. She had been in conversation with the middle-aged stranger on the opposite side of the room for over an hour.

The Pastor returned a moment later. He walked around behind the Marvels and got down on one knee. They turned towards him.

"This isn't going to be easy," he said.

"What do you mean," asked Mr. Marvel. His wife gripped his hand.

"That man with Officer Murdock? You see him?"

"Sure, of course, I saw him come in with her an hour ago. Who is he?"

The Pastor laid a hand on each of their shoulders. "That's the man who hit your son," he said.

Mrs. Marvel gasped, and put both hands on her face. Her husband tensed and anger flared in his eyes. The man who hit their son. Right here with them as they patiently and prayerfully waited for the 'No Admittance' doors to open and for the doctor to emerge with news.

Mr. Marvel didn't know what to do. Officer Murdock had made it clear that the driver was not at fault in the accident; in fact, he did everything he could to prevent it. Still, he was the person who had just turned their world upside down, perhaps forever.

Only moments before, the group had shared the remarkable contents of Jonathan Marvel's

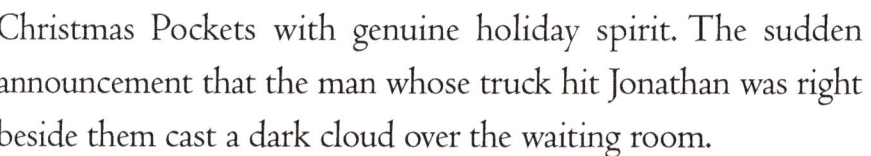

Christmas Pockets with genuine holiday spirit. The sudden announcement that the man whose truck hit Jonathan was right beside them cast a dark cloud over the waiting room.

The Pastor waited in silence behind them. He could only imagine how difficult this moment was for them.

"You don't want us to TALK to the man, do you?" Mr. Marvel finally asked the Pastor. "My God, how could we?"

"If you want to drag my God into this," replied the Pastor, "I think you know what He would have to say."

Mr. Marvel looked at his wife. She could not bring herself to say anything. She looked down at the floor. This was a decision she could not—would not—make.

Mr. Marvel looked at the people who had brought comfort and support to him and his wife all this long, terrible day. They had no idea what he had just been asked to do.

His eyes swept across the room, from the Yees to Felipe and his mother, from the teacher and the babysitter to old Mr. Cowl. He saw something in their expressions that began to still the rage that welled up inside when he learned that the man who sent his son to the hospital was right here in the room. He saw hope. He saw caring. He saw belonging. And he saw love.

"I'm not sure I can do this," he said to the Pastor.

"Whatever happens in that surgery tonight, lives will be changed forever," the Pastor replied. "We don't talk a lot about miracles anymore. Maybe we should. I've been at this business for a long time, but before tonight I'm not sure I could tell you if I've ever seen anything that looks even remotely like a miracle."

The Pastor laid his hand gently on Mrs. Marvel's back. "Look around, both of you. Look at the people who have come together tonight in this room. Some friends, some strangers—at least before tonight. It all changed tonight."

He let that thought sink in for a minute.

"And now, for the miracle. A small one perhaps, but a miracle nonetheless. Look at Jonathan's coat. Look at those silly, wonderful pockets. Think of the thought and time and care that went into engineering that coat. And the gifts? The absolutely perfect gifts, just right for each person who received one, just what they needed right now, tonight, on Christmas Eve. The Three Wise men themselves could not have done any   better if they had been asked to select gifts for this group of people."

The Pastor took Mrs. Marvel's hand. "But that's not the miracle, is it. Not the coat. It was just the vehicle to deliver the miracle. No, the miracle is something else, isn't it."

Mrs. Marvel looked out at the people who surrounded them, the friends who had been with them all day. The people for whom Jonathan had so lovingly and carefully planned. The people! That was it.

"It's the people," she said excitedly. "All of them. All of them here, right now."

Her husband's brow wrinkled. "The people? I'm not sure I get it."

Mrs. Marvel stood up. She ran a hand through her hair. She looked at the Pastor, and his eyes were shining. She was right.

Their friends didn't know what to make of the conversation: a miracle? With Jonathan still lying on a surgical table, his fate unknown, the possibility of his death a real and immediate possibility? What kind of miracle was that?

Mrs. Marvel waved her hand around the room. "Don't you see? "she asked her husband. "Every single person who has a pocket on Jonathan's coat is right here in this room! They didn't know they were getting gifts. How could they? And they didn't all have to come here today, either. How did they know? What was it that brought each of them here?"

She sat down, feeling exhausted and a little exhilarated. Mr. Cowl smiled at her, and even gave her a wink.

"You're all here," she said to the group of people waiting with her.

Then she pointed up to the cross above the door leading into the surgery.

"And He is here," she finished.

The Pastor planted a kiss on Mrs. Marvel's cheek.

Mr. Marvel said, "Your little miracle is missing an important piece." He held up the last envelope from Jonathan's coat, the one that was addressed to '*The Person Who Needs A Present The Most Today.*'

"Who is this for? Everyone here received something….- except for Officer Murdock. Was this meant for her? Is she the one who needs a gift more than the rest of of us?"

"I can answer that," said the Officer, who had quietly come up to the group as Mrs. Marvel was talking about miracles.

"It's not for me. I don't need it….what I have shared here today with all of you is one of the greatest Christmas gifts I can imagine receiving. So, thanks, but that envelope isn't for me."

The waiting room became still as family and friends thought about the day's events, especially what had transpired in the last half hour as Jonathan Marvel's Christmas Pockets had been opened and the gifts distributed.

But one gift remained. Who was it for?

Mr. Marvel looked at the Pastor. He did not see what he expected: concern, frustration or even unhappiness about his 'little miracle' theory being proven wrong. In fact, what he saw surprised him enough that he nudged his wife and pointed in the Pastor's direction.

"What's up?" he whispered.

She looked across the room at the Pastor, who had walked over to the table that was decorated with the Nativity scene. He looked anything but frustrated; in fact, he looked downright cheerful. She joined him and they spoke for a minute. When they retruned, Jonathan Marvel's mother was smiling.

"I give," said her husband. "Why the smile?"

She gestured to the Pastor. He picked up the cue.

"You're wrong about there being one person missing from Jonathan's list," said Pastor. "They are all here. Every one of them."

"Even the person who needs a gift more than anyone else today?" asked Mr. Marvel.

"Especially that person," replied the Pastor.

Pastor nodded to Officer Murdock. She walked over to the Emergency room door and motioned to someone waiting outside. The door slid open and the man whose truck hit Jonathan Marvel in front of Yee's grocery store earlier that day walked in.

No one had noticed him leaving a few minutes earlier, or seen Officer Murdock follow him out to the parking area.

The middle-aged man shuffled across the room and stood directly in front of the Marvels. A weathered baseball cap was wedged tightly in his hands.

The man did not look at the Marvels at first. When he finally spoke, his voice was beyond sorrowful. It was the voice of a man broken to his core.

"I truly do not know what to say to you," he began. "I only wish I could take this day back. I wish it was me that was back in that room, and not your boy. I had a wife and a boy once. I know what it is like to lose the people you love the most."

He raised his head, and looked at Mrs. Marvel. "No, I would not wish that pain on any human being."

Was it absolution the man sought from them, Mr. Marvel wondered—or punishment?

Then in a voice much calmer than she imagined she could speak with Mrs. Marvel asked, "What is your name?"

The softness of her voice jolted the man. He did not expect this.

"William, ma'am. My name is William."

"Won't you sit down please, William," she said. Mr. Yee pulled a chair over, and William sat down in front of the Marvels.

"Officer Murdock explained what happened today," said Mr. Marvel. "We know it wasn't your fault, and that you tried as best you could to get out of the way."

William had one hand planted firmly on each knee. "I did," he said, "I surely did try." A quiet sob welled up inside him. "Lord knows, I did try."

"Each of us here in this room has a special kind of connection with Jonathan," Mrs. Marvel said.

"And because of that connection he got this crazy idea to make a special gift for each one of us, and to deliver the presents today with his own special flair." She held up Jonathan's overcoat.

"Them pockets," said William. "I saw you all talking about them."

"I don't know how Jonathan knew exactly what it was that we each needed this Christmas," she continued. "But he got it just right for everybody."

Heads nodded all around the room.

Mr. Marvel picked up the conversation. "There was one pocket that Jonathan did not have a definite person in mind for. The gift inside is supposed to go the person who needs it more than anybody else today."

William's lips pursed, and he shook his head. This was all beyond his understanding.

"We owe you an apology, William," said Mrs. Marvel. "We should have figured out a lot sooner who it was who needed Jonathan's most remarkable gift."

She reached onto the chair beside her and picked up the last envelope.

"Please, take it," she said.

William accepted the envelope.

"I don't know what to say," William replied. "Guess I already said that once."

Mr. Marvel chuckled. "Welcome to the club, William. We've all been in that pickle today."

Felipe spoke up. "Read what's inside; that's what we all did with our presents from Jonathan."

William looked at the Marvels. "Please," said Mrs. Marvel.

He opened the envelope, and unfolded the sheet of paper inside.

"Well, it has a picture on it that says 'Jonathan,'" began William. He held the picture high so everyone could see. It featured a drawing of a boy who was flexing his muscles outside on a bright, sunny day.

"What does it say underneath?" asked the teacher.

"Let me see here," said William. He cleared his throat—twice—and began to read Jonathan's message:

"Dear friend,
I'm sorry I don't know your name yet, but I hope we can meet someday."

William stopped reading. He bowed his head, and began to weep. The babysitter, who was seated next to him, gently took the paper from his hands and continued reading:

"My mom and dad always tell me how we are blessed to have the simple things like food and a house to live in, plus we have friends and people who love us, too. I don't have a lot of stuff, but I know my mom would make something for you to eat and my dad is really good at fixing cars and stuff if that helps you.

Mostly I am good at being a friend. That's why I drew this picture of me in my backyard. It's where I like to play. Anyway, I hope you remember me if you want to have a new friend or maybe some dinner with us. You are welcome at our house.

Your new friend, Jonathan.

PS: Did I say Merry Christmas?"

The babysitter finished reading, folded the paper and handed it to William.

❄ 10 ❄

The people waiting for news about Jonathan Marvel drifted into quite conversations. Then a door opened, and once again the sound of Christmas music floated into the waiting room. Mr. Cowl stood up to stretch and the Yees began piling more cookies and donuts on trays. A new admitting nurse came on shift and a lab technician wheeled his bike through the entry door and down the hallway where the music was playing.

William went over to the counter to pour a cup of coffee, and Grandmother Marvel pulled out her crochet needles and began giving the babysitter another lesson. Jonathan's teacher was playing a word game on a pad of paper with Felipe and his mother.

Mr. and Mrs. Marvel were so engaged in conversation with the Pastor that they didn't notice the wide door under the 'No Admittance' sign swing open.

Someone said, "Can anybody join this party?"

The Marvels and their Pastor turned around and found themselves face-to-face with Jonathan's doctor. He did not look at all like a man who had performed two extraordinarily difficult surgeries that day. The smile that spread across his face said something else altogether.

Mrs. Marvel didn't wait for the words; she threw herself into the doctor's open arms and gave him a long hug.

"Jonathan is going to be fine," said the doctor. "Good as new in fact."

Twelve people, faces beaming, swarmed around the doctor and the Marvels. Even Mr. Cowl couldn't resist a show of happiness; he slapped William on the back so hard that his coffee spilled.

Both men just laughed.

"The hematoma subsided, in some part on its own," said the doctor. "They do that sometimes, it's the darnedest thing. For now, Jonathan is sedated, and he will be until tomorrow afternoon.

"He is being moved to a room where you can visit, and if you ask for a roll-away bed, I'm sure the nursing staff can take care of that, too."

He pointed to Jonathan's overcoat lying on the table in front of the Marvels' chairs, and grinned.

"I've just never seen anything like that," he said.

"And you won't ever again—none of us will," said the Pastor. "That's the way it is with miracles. They don't repeat themselves."

"Then I'll be praying for a brand new miracle with my next patient," said the doctor.

He looked at the clock on the wall. "And that's only a few hours from now.

Time to go. Merry Christmas to you all."

The doctor shook hands all around and hugged Mrs. Marvel again before opening the door behind the reception desk and vanishing from their lives.

Jonathan Marvel's friends, old and new, gathered their belongings, said Merry Christmas and goodbye to one another, and walked out into the still Christmas night.

Mr. Marvel gave William their home address and phone number, and asked him to call so that he could meet Jonathan when he came home. Mrs. Marvel did the same with Felipe and his mother, and together the Marvels cornered Mr. Cowl and told him in no uncertain terms that he WAS to come to the belated Christmas dinner they would have when Jonathan felt better. The old man did not argue. The Yees offered to drive Grandmother Marvel home, and in a minute, the Marvels and their Pastor were alone in the hospital waiting room.

"Quiet night for the hospital," said the Pastor.

"Maybe that was part of your small miracle?" asked Mr. Marvel.

"I'd like to think so."

The Pastor helped the Marvels pick up their things. He handed Jonathan's remarkable Christmas coat to Mrs. Marvel and asked, "Are you still going to throw it away?"

There were tears in Mrs. Marvel's eyes. She shook her head, smiled, and then kissed him and handed back the note Jonathan had written to him.

The Pastor walked Jonathan's mother and father to the door under the sign that said 'No Admittance,' and prayed for them as the door swung open. Then he watched as they disappeared down the corridor to begin the next adventure in Jonathan Marvel's life.

Pastor looked around the empty waiting room. He checked to see that his own special gift from Jonathan Marvel's Christmas Pockets was safely in his jacket, waved to the admitting nurse behind the glass window, and pushed the button to open the sliding doors and exit the hospital.

He stepped out into the cold, starry night, and breathed deeply. Then a thought struck him and he turned to go back into the hospital.

The clock on the wall said 2:20 AM. He went over to the table that was decorated with the Nativity scene and Christmas tree.

"Merry Christmas," said the Pastor as he laid Jonathan's gift for the baby Jesus under the tree.

He looked up at the cross above the door that lead to Jonathan's room.

"And thanks," he added, before buttoning his jacket collar and heading out into the night.

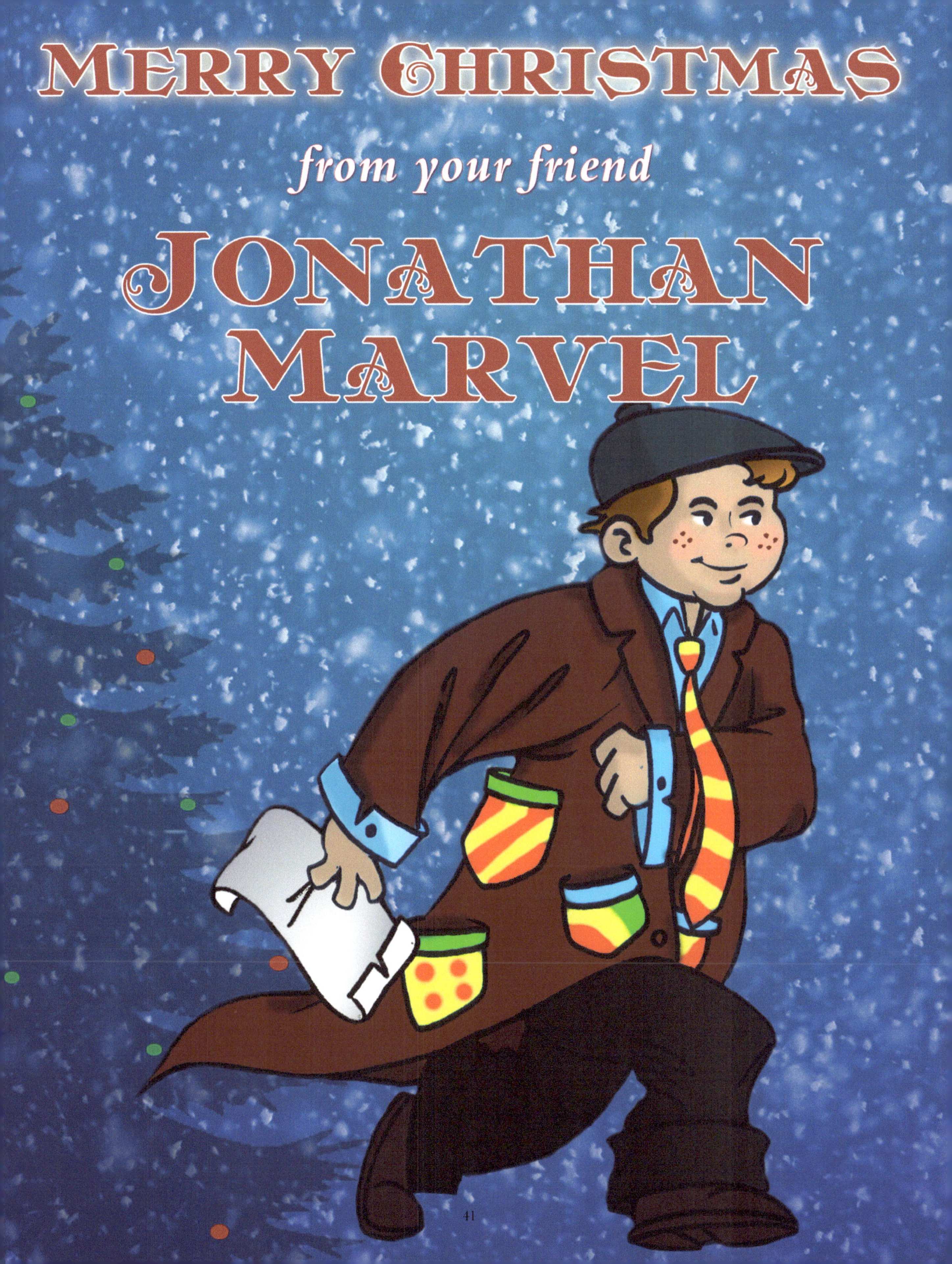

MERRY CHRISTMAS

from your friend

JONATHAN MARVEL

B.R. O'Hagan lives in the rural Willamette Valley of Oregon, in a landscape of vineyards, forests and farms. He has written for film and television, and, under his pen names, has authored 23 books. *Jonathan Marvel's Christmas Pockets* and his upcoming historical fiction series mark his return to writing under his given name, a decision that has made it easier for his wife Lesli and daughter Natalie Elizabeth to remember what to call him on any given day.

B.R. is a graduate of UCLA who writes in a converted barn. In the winter he splits seasoned oak and Douglas fir for the wood stove that heats his farmhouse, and in the summer he tries to keep up with everything growing in and around the pasture.

The idea for Jonathan Marvel grew out of a challenge to add an entirely new Christmas story to the library of 'standard' holiday tales we all enjoy, and from the author's abiding belief in the greatest story ever told. The gifts from *His* Christmas pockets are without end.

———————

Pedee Creek Press

Hilton Head Island, South Carolina

info@brohagan.com

www.ingramcontent.com/pod-product-compliance
Lightning Source LLC
Chambersburg PA
CBHW041012170626
46815CB00003B/264